RUSSELL, GRUNT AND SNORT

For Jack and Reuben - J.C.

RUSSELL,
GRUNT AND
SNORT
A RED FOX
BOOK
978-1782
955627

Published in Great Britain by Red Fox,
an imprint of Random House Children's Publishers UK
A Random House Group Company This edition published 2013
10 9 8 7 6 5 4 3 2 1 Copyright © Jason Chapman, 2013
The right of Jason Chapman to be identified as the author of this work
has been asserted in accordance with the Copyright, Designs and
Patents Act 1988. All rights reserved. No part of this publication may be
reproduced, stored in a retrieval system, or transmitted in any form
or by any means, electronic, mechanical, photocopying,
recording or otherwise, without the prior permission of the publishers.
Red Fox Books are published by Random House Children's
Publishers UK, 61–63 Uxbridge Road, London W5 5SA
www.randomhousechildrens.co.uk   www.randomhouse.co.uk
Addresses for companies within The Random House Group Limited
can be found at: www.randomhouse.co.uk/offices.htm
THE RANDOM HOUSE GROUP Limited Reg. No. 954009
A CIP catalogue record for this book is available
from the British Library.
Printed in China

Jason Chapman

RUSSELL, GRUNT AND SNORT

RED FOX

On a moonlit night in a muddy field, three pigs looked out to sea.
"I'm not sure . . ." said Russell, thinking aloud, "that this is the
right place for me."

For a long time now he'd thought and thought, and
thought some more . . . *What's beyond the water?*
Where do those boats go?

Ever since piglethood, Russell had wondered about life on the other side.

"There must be a life," said Russell, "a life in a perfect place with all the apples and truffles a pig could eat."

But any pig who'd ever wondered if life was better outside the field had never made it past the zappy fence.

"Come to bed, Russell," said Grunt. "You'll feel much better in the morning."

But in the morning Russell didn't feel better.

Not when he woke up with
rain dripping on his head, again,

nor when he tripped and fell face
first into the stinky mud, again,

nor when the farmer threw half a
scoop of pig nuts into the trough for
breakfast, again. Russell sighed.

Enough, he thought to himself.

All that day, Russell behaved very oddly.

He scurried around the field picking up all the pignuts he could find.

He broke branches from trees and untwisted twine from the hedges.

He measured the curve on the roof of the house and paced across the field counting his steps.

What is he up to? thought the other pigs.

That evening as the sun went down, Russell told Grunt and Snort about his plan to escape.

"You're a genius," said Grunt.

"You're potty," said Snort.

"Right, then," said Russell, "after three. One, two, three . . ."

Singing a song, they sailed off into the sunset . . .

"Three piggies went to sea, sea, sea
to see what they could see, see, see,
but all that they could see, see, see
was the bottom of the deep blue sea, sea, sea."

The three pigs sailed for a day and a night until they were rudely awoken by the deafening horn of the *Fat Princess*, the biggest cruise ship in the world.

HAAAUUNNGG!

They scaled the side of the massive ship and scuttled around the decks looking for somewhere to hide.

Russell, Grunt and Snort found some clothes and tried to mingle with the guests. They played Snap in the casino,

drank banana milkshakes by the pool,

and went ballroom dancing.

But when they were invited to dine with the captain,
Russell knew something wasn't right.

"GO! GO! GO!!" he shrieked. "This is no place for a pig!" Luckily the *Fat Princess* had docked and they ran from the ship as fast as their trotters could take them.

They jumped on a rickshaw and headed for the hills.
"Keep pedalling, Grunt," said Snort.

Russell, Grunt and Snort pedalled deep into the heart of the jungle and then got a bit lost. Luckily, a tiger and a bear were out for an evening stroll. They took the three pigs back to meet their friends.

Grunt and Snort told the animals about their muddy field and their great escape.

"My dear pigs," said the lion, "you must stay here with us. At least join us for . . . dinner." Grunt and Snort beamed with delight, but Russell knew something wasn't right.

"RUN! RUN! RUN!!"

squealed Russell.
"This is no place for a pig!"
Never before had the three pigs run so fast.

"Taxi turtles at your service," called a voice from the water's edge.

"No journey too near or too far."

"Full steam ahead, taxi turtles," said Russell.

Several surfing hours later, the pigs reached a beach.
Finding a pile of clothes, they quickly dressed and trotted
up to the nearby train station.

The hours rolled past and the train sped on. But suddenly. . .

The pigs didn't have a ticket so the ticket inspector suggested they
assist the prize-winning chef, Monsieur Boucher, in the dining carriage.
Yet again, Russell knew something wasn't right.

"**JUMP! JUMP! JUMP!!**"

yelled Russell. "This is no place for a pig!" and the pigs rolled down the hill, ending up in a wet and muddy bog.

"Oh, mud," said Russell, "how I've missed you."
Exhausted, the pigs curled up together and slept long, deep sleeps.

At dawn the next morning a dreadful thing happened.
Russell woke with a start at the sound of rusty brakes, the slam
of a door and the bark of a dog. Before you could say, "knife",
the three tired pigs were herded into the back of a truck.

"I've got a really bad feeling about this," said Grunt.

"It looks like the end of the road," said Snort.

"I'm really sorry," whispered Russell.

"This is all my fault for wanting a better life."

The lorry went up hills and down dales and stopped
at a large building. The three pigs were led through
a door to a large room with lots of other pigs.

"This is a bit cosy," said Grunt.

"A bit too cosy," said Snort.

"DIG! DIG! DIG!!" cried Russell. "This is no place for a pig!"
And the pigs did what pigs do best . . . DIG!

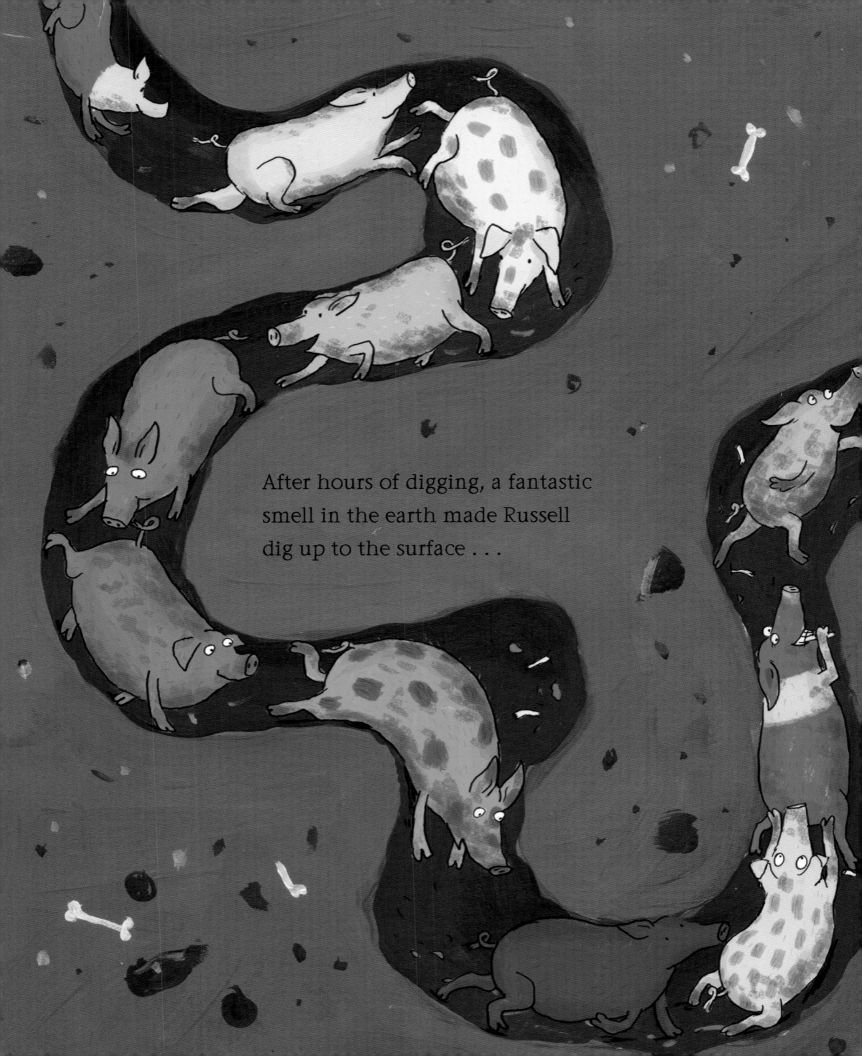

After hours of digging, a fantastic
smell in the earth made Russell
dig up to the surface . . .

"Apples and truffles," squealed Russell, as he climbed
out of the tunnel into an undiscovered old oak wood.
"All the apples and truffles a pig could eat," said Grunt.
"Russell, you made the dream come true!" said Snort,
with tears in her eyes.

"This," said Russell, tossing apples in the air,
"is the perfect place for a pig like me."

This Little Tiger book belongs to:

_____

_____

_____

_____

For Deborah
~ *DB*

For Noah who is little, and
for Jake who wants to be BIG
~ *JC*

LITTLE TIGER PRESS
An imprint of Magi Publications
1 The Coda Centre, 189 Munster Road, London SW6 6AW
www.littletigerpress.com
This paperback edition published in 2001
First published in Great Britain 2001
Text © 2001 David Bedford • Illustrations © 2001 Jane Chapman
David Bedford and Jane Chapman have asserted their rights to be
identified as the author and illustrator of this work under the
Copyright, Designs and Patents Act, 1988.
Printed in Belgium by Proost NV, Turnhout
5 7 9 10 8 6 4

Big Bear
Little Bear

David Bedford and Jane Chapman

Little Tiger Press

London

One bright cold morning Little Bear helped
Mother Bear scoop snow out of their den.
"This will make more room for you to play,"
said Mother Bear. "You're getting bigger now."

"I want to be as big as you when I'm grown up,"
said Little Bear. He stretched up his arms and
made himself as big as he could.

Mother Bear stretched to the sky.
"You'll have to eat and eat to be
as big as I am," she said.
"When I'm big, I'll wrestle you
in the snow," said Little Bear.
Wrestling in the snow was
his favourite game.

"You're not big enough to wrestle me yet,"
said Mother Bear, laughing.
She rolled Little Bear over and over in
the soft snow and Little Bear giggled.

Little Bear shook the snow from his fur.
"When I'm grown up I want to run as
fast as you, Mummy," he said.
"You'll have to practise if you want to
be as fast as I am," said Mother Bear.

Little Bear darted away and
ran as fast as he could . . .

but his mother soon caught up with him.
"Run faster!" she called.
"I can't," said Little Bear. "I'm not grown
up yet."

"I'll show you what it's like to be grown up," said Mother Bear. "Climb on to my shoulders!" When Little Bear stood on his mother's shoulders he could see to the end of the world, and when he reached up his hands he could nearly touch the sky. "Now you *are* big," said Mother Bear.

"Let's run," cried Mother Bear, and she
ran faster and faster.
Little Bear felt the wind rushing against
his face and blowing his ears back.
"This is how I'll run when I'm grown up,"
he shouted.

Suddenly, Mother Bear leapt into the air.
Little Bear saw the world rushing under him.
"I'm flying like a bird," he shouted.
Then he saw where they were going to land . . .

SPLASH!

Mother Bear dived into the cold water and swam along with Little Bear on her back. "This is how you'll swim when you're grown up," she said.

Little Bear watched his mother
carefully so he would know
what to do next time.
"I'll soon be able to swim like
that," he told himself.

Mother Bear
climbed out of
the water with
Little Bear still
clinging tightly
to her back.
"Will I *really* be as
big as you when
I'm grown up?"
asked Little Bear.

"Yes you will,"
said his mother -
"but I don't want
you to grow up yet."
"Why not?" asked
Little Bear.

"You won't be able to sit on my shoulders when you're grown up," said Mother Bear, as she carried Little Bear back to their snow den.

Little Bear was tired after wrestling,
running, flying and swimming.
"You can still cuddle me when
I'm grown up," he said, sleepily.
"But Mummy," he whispered,
"I don't want to grow up yet."

"That's good," said Mother Bear,
holding him close, "because . . .

you're perfect just the way
you are."
Little Bear snuggled into his
mother's soft fur, and they
went to sleep together in
their cosy den in the snow.

It's grrreat to read titles like these

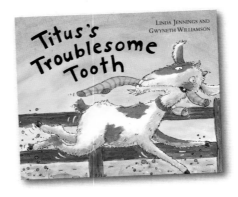

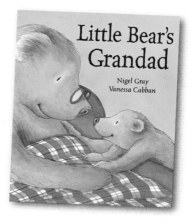

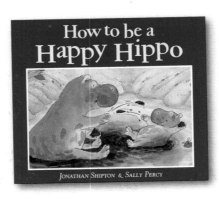

For information regarding any of the above titles or for our catalogue, please contact:
Little Tiger Press, 1 The Coda Centre, 189 Munster Road, London SW6 6AW, UK
Telephone: 020 7385 6333 Fax: 020 7385 7333 e-mail: info@littletiger.co.uk